SPACE BOY

FOR MARK

www.houghtonmifflinbooks.com

The text of this book is set in GrenadineMVB.

The illustrations are watercolor and pencil on paper.

Library of Congress Cataloging-in-Publication Data

Landry, Leo.
Space boy / written and illustrated by Leo Landry.
p. cm.
Summary: Having decided not to go to bed because his home is too noisy, Nicholas
flies his spaceship to the moon, where he enjoys a snack, takes a moonwalk, and
enjoys the quiet—until he realizes what he is missing at home.
ISBN-13: 978-0-618-60568-2 (hardcover)
ISBN-10: 0-618-60568-1 (hardcover)
[1. Noise—Fiction. 2. Bedtime—Fiction. 3. Moon—Fiction. 4. Family life—Fiction. 5.
Space flight to the moon—Fiction.] I. Title.
PZ7.L2317357Spa 2007
[E]—dc22
2006026081

Printed in Singapore
TWP 10 9 8 7 6 5 4 3 2 1

SPACE BOY

WRITTEN AND ILLUSTRATED BY LEO LANDRY

HOUGHTON MIFFLIN COMPANY
BOSTON 2007

The moon shined brightly as Nicholas readied for bed.

This is what he could hear:

his baby sister crying in her crib,

the dog barking to be let out,

and the radio blaring on the front porch.

Even the noises from his neighborhood floated through his open window.

Too loud, thought Nicholas, holding his ears, *and I'm NOT going to bed!*

In that moment, Nicholas made a decision.

He tiptoed quietly to the kitchen.
He packed two cheese and tomato sandwiches,
one bottle of water, a bunch of grapes, and a cookie.
He fit the food nicely into his lunch box along with a napkin.

Next, Nicholas got dressed. First he climbed into his space suit. Then he put on his space boots. At last he put on his space helmet. Nicholas read his list aloud to make sure he was ready.

Then Nicholas walked outside to the backyard and climbed into his rocket.

He strapped himself in and prepared for takeoff.
Nicholas knew exactly which buttons to push, and when
to push them. "Four . . . three . . . two . . . one . . . liftoff!"
he shouted. The rocket soared into space.

Nicholas turned and looked out the window.

Below, he could see the noisy world slowly fall away.

Above, he saw the moon.

Almost there, he thought.

The rocket touched down gently on the lunar surface.
Nicholas opened the hatch, climbed down the ladder,
and stepped onto the cold, dusty landscape.

It was *so* quiet on the moon.

This is what Nicholas could *not* hear:
his baby sister crying,
the dog barking,
or the radio blaring.

How nice, thought Nicholas.
He spread out his blanket and unpacked his snack.

The lack of gravity was a problem. The tomato slices rose softly into the atmosphere.

They looked as big and round as the earth as they slowly floated away.

Nicholas held on to his sandwich and ate what was left.
He ate his grapes, took a sip of water, and saved his cookie
for last. *"Delicious!"* he said to himself.

When he had finished, Nicholas went for a moonwalk.
He bounded across huge craters and scaled miniature mountains.
The beautiful blue earth appeared behind every peak, silent and peaceful.

As Nicholas walked, he looked back at his footprints in the soft lunar surface. *Just like footprints at the beach,* he thought, remembering how he had helped his baby sister take her very first steps toward the ocean in the cool wet sand.

Nicholas continued his walk. The vast, wide-open spaces on the moon reminded him of his dog.

Wouldn't he just love to run and run and run, with no end in sight? Nicholas thought. *Though he would probably miss the green grass in our yard.*

And seeing the earth again, Nicholas remembered those warm summer nights when his family sat out on the porch in the light of the full moon.

This moon.

His moonwalk had brought him back to his spaceship.
Back up the ladder went Nicholas. He climbed
through the hatch and strapped himself in.
"Four . . . three . . . two . . . one . . . liftoff!" he shouted.

The rocket soared into space. Nicholas could see the craters and valleys of the silent moon slowly fall away.

Ahead, he saw the earth.

Soon the rocket touched down gently in his backyard. Nicholas opened the hatch, climbed down the ladder, and stepped onto the moonlit grass.

He went into his room and took off his space suit,
his space helmet, and his space boots. He tiptoed
gently down the hallway.

This is what Nicholas could see:

his baby sister sleeping in her crib,

the dog curled snugly in his bed, and

his parents sitting together on the porch, listening to the radio.
It was a lovely evening in his neighborhood.

"I'm ready for bed now," Nicholas told his parents. "Good night."

"Good night, Nicholas," said his parents.

It was good to be home.